D0909277

A Note to Parents and Caregivers:

Read-it! Joke Books are for children who are moving ahead on the amazing road to reading. These fun books support the acquisition and extension of reading skills as well as a love of books.

Published by the same company that produces *Read-it!* Readers, these books introduce the question/answer and dialogue patterns that help children expand their thinking about language structure and book formats.

When sharing joke books with a child, read in short stretches. Pause often to talk about the meaning of the jokes. The question/answer and dialogue formats work well for this purpose and provide an opportunity to talk about the language and meaning of the jokes. Have the child turn the pages and point to the pictures and familiar words. When you read the jokes, have fun creating the voices of characters or emphasizing some important words. Be sure to reread favorite jokes.

There is no right or wrong way to share books with children. Find time to read with your child, and pass on the legacy of literacy.

Adria F. Klein, Ph.D.
Professor Emeritus
California State University
San Bernardino, California

Managing Editors: Bob Temple, Catherine Neitge
Creative Director: Terri Foley
Editors: Jerry Ruff, Christianne Jones
Designer: Les Tranby
Page production: Picture Window Books
The illustrations in this book were rendered digitally.

Picture Window Books
5115 Excelsior Boulevard
Suite 232
Minneapolis, MN 55416
877-845-8392
www.picturewindowbooks.com

Printed in the United States of America.

Library of Congress Cataloging-in-Publication Data
Moore, Mark, 1947-
Chalkboard chuckles : a book of classroom jokes / by Mark Moore ;
illustrated by Anne Haberstroh.
p. cm. — (Read-it! joke books—supercharged!)
ISBN 1-4048-0626-1
1. Schools—Juvenile humor. 2. Education—Juvenile humor. 3. Wit
and humor, Juvenile. I. Title. II. Series.

PN6231.S3M68 2004
818'.602—dc22   2004007322

Chalkboard Chuckles

A Book of Classroom Jokes

By Mark Moore • Illustrated by Anne Haberstroh

Reading Advisers:
Adria F. Klein, Ph.D.
Professor Emeritus, California State University
San Bernardino, California

Susan Kesselring, M.A., Literacy Educator
Rosemount-Apple Valley-Eagan (Minnesota) School District

PiCTURE WiNDOW BOOKS
Minneapolis, Minnesota

What's the hardest thing about falling out of bed the first day of school?

The floor.

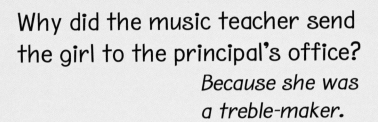

Why did the music teacher send
the girl to the principal's office?

*Because she was
a treble-maker.*

Teacher:

"Where's the capital
in Missouri?"

Student:

"The M."

How did the music teacher
unlock her secrets?

With piano keys.

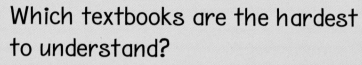

Which textbooks are the hardest to understand?

Math books because they have so many problems.

First student:
"Who gave you that black eye?"
Second student:
"Nobody gave it to me.
I had to fight for it."

What's black all over but gets white when it's dirty?

A chalkboard.

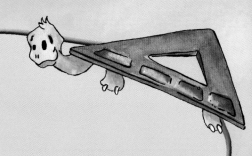

Teacher:
  "Now, be sure to go
    straight home."
Student:
  "I can't."
Teacher:
  "Why not?"
Student:
  "Because I live around
    the corner."

What happened to the
school plumber?
  He went down the drain.

Why did the pony have to stay after school?

> *For horsing around.*

Teacher:
> "This is the fifth time this week you haven't had your homework."

Student:
> "Good thing it's Friday!"

Why are some fish so smart?

> *They spend their whole lives in schools.*

How do monsters
get to school?

On a ghoul bus.

Why did the teacher
wear sunglasses?
> *Because her students
> were so bright.*

Why did the principal marry
the janitor?
> *Because he swept
> her off her feet.*

Why did the computer have so
many dents?
> *Because it was
> always crashing.*

Why did the student take a job in the school bakery?

Because she wanted to loaf around.

Why did the teacher send the clock to the principal's office?

Because it was taking too much time.

What do you call a student with an encyclopedia in her pocket?

Smarty pants.

What did the magnet
say to the paper clip?

I'm attracted to you.

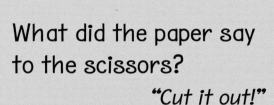

What did the paper say
to the scissors?

"Cut it out!"

What kind of shoes do
lazy students wear?

Loafers.

Why did the music student bring
a ladder to class?

Because the teacher asked
him to sing higher.

Why did the kids give Jimmy
a dog bone?

*Because he was
the teacher's pet.*

Teacher:

"Jessica, you're late. You should
have been here an hour ago."

Jessica:

"Why? What happened?"

What happened to make the little
broom late for school?

He overswept.

Why did the football coach send in his second string?

> So he could tie up the game.

Why did the girl bring a ladder to graduation?

> Because she was going on to high school.

Teacher:
   "Why do they call it
   a litter of puppies?"
Student:
   "Because they are so messy!"

Why was the school soccer team so successful?

Because it was goal-oriented.

What happens when you stare at chalk writing too long?

You get really board.

Where does the third grade come after the fourth grade?

In the dictionary.

Where's the best place to learn how to make ice cream?

At sundae school.

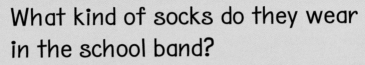

What kind of socks do they wear
in the school band?

> *Tuba socks.*

Danny:
> "I ain't got my homework."

Teacher:
> "I don't have my homework."

Danny:
> "Well, that makes both of us."

Why did Jimmy do so well on
the geometry test?

> *Because he knew
> all the angles.*

What's black and white
and read all over?

The pages of a textbook.

Teacher:

"Order, class! Order!"

Student:

"I'll have a hamburger
and fries, please."

Why did the school cook
bake bread?

*Because he kneaded
the dough.*

19

Teacher:
    "Mary, did your Dad help
    with your homework?"
Mary:
    "No."
Teacher:
    "Are you sure?"
Mary:
    "Honest. He did it all by himself."

Why is history always getting harder?

Because new things happen every day.

Teacher:
"I thought I sent you to the back of the line."
Student:
"I know, but someone else was already there."

What did the glue say to the paper?

I'm stuck on you.

21

Teacher:

"Students, you have 10 minutes for each question on the test."

Student:

"How long do we have for each answer?"

What lies on its back, raises 44 smelly feet, grunts, and sweats?

Gym class.

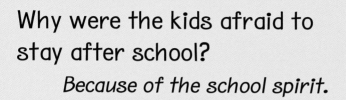

Why were the kids afraid to stay after school?

> *Because of the school spirit.*

Why did the history teacher go out with the principal?

> *Because she loved dates.*

What happens when you fail the final exam in history class?

> *History repeats itself.*

Look for all of the books in this series:

Read-it! Joke Books—Supercharged!

Beastly Laughs
A Book of Monster Jokes

Chalkboard Chuckles
A Book of Classroom Jokes

Creepy Crawlers
A Book of Bug Jokes

Roaring with Laughter
A Book of Animal Jokes

Sit! Stay! Laugh!
A Book of Pet Jokes

Spooky Sillies
A Book of Ghost Jokes

Read-it! Joke Books

Alphabet Soup
A Book of Riddles About Letters

Animal Quack-Ups
Foolish and Funny Jokes About Animals

Bell Buzzers
A Book of Knock-Knock Jokes

Chewy Chuckles
Deliciously Funny Jokes About Food

Crazy Criss-Cross
A Book of Mixed-Up Riddles

Ding Dong
A Book of Knock-Knock Jokes

Dino Rib Ticklers
Hugely Funny Jokes About Dinosaurs

Doctor, Doctor
A Book of Doctor Jokes

Door Knockers
A Book of Knock-Knock Jokes

Family Funnies
A Book of Family Jokes

Funny Talk
A Book of Silly Riddles

Galactic Giggles
Far-Out and Funny Jokes About Outer Space

Laughs on a Leash
A Book of Pet Jokes

Monster Laughs
Frightfully Funny Jokes About Monsters

Nutty Neighbors
A Book of Knock-Knock Jokes

Open Up and Laugh!
A Book of Knock-Knock Jokes

Rhyme Time
A Book of Rhyming Riddles

School Buzz
Classy and Funny Jokes About School

School Daze
A Book of Riddles About School

Teacher Says
A Book of Teacher Jokes

Three-Alarm Jokes
A Book of Firefighter Jokes

Under Arrest
A Book of Police Jokes

Who's There?
A Book of Knock-Knock Jokes

Zoodles
A Book of Riddles About Animals